6/12

*Dear Parent:*
*Your child's love of reading starts here*

Every child learns to read in a different way and at his or her own speed. Some go back and forth between reading levels and read favorite books again and again. Others read through each level in order. You can help your young reader improve and become more confident by encouraging his or her own interests and abilities. From books your child reads with you to the first books he or she reads alone, there are I Can Read Books for every stage of reading:

**My First**

**SHARED READING**
Basic language, word repetition, and whimsical illustrations, ideal for sharing with your emergent reader

**1**

**BEGINNING READING**
Short sentences, familiar words, and simple concepts
for ch

**2**

REA
Engag
for de

**DATE DUE**

ay

**3**

REA
Comp
for th

terest topics

**4**

ADV
Short
for th

I Can Read
since 1957. Fe
fabulous cast
standard for k

of reading
rs and a
the

A lifetime of

Can Read!"

*—For Andrew-Blandrew*
*—M.C.*


*—For Josephine,*
*who can read this!*
*—R.N.*

HarperCollins® and I Can Read Book® are trademarks of HarperCollins Publishers.

Library of Congress Cataloging-in-Publication Data
Cuyler, Margery.
    Tick tock clock / by Margery Cuyler ; [illustrations by Robert Neubecker]. — 1st ed.
        p.    cm. — (My first I can read book)
    Summary: As the hours tick by from nine in the morning to seven at night, two rambunctious twins create mayhem.
    ISBN 978-0-06-136309-2 (trade bdg.) — ISBN 978-0-06-136311-5 (pbk.)
    [1. Stories in rhyme.   2. Time—Fiction.   3. Twins—Fiction.   4. Brothers and sisters—Fiction.]   I. Neubecker, Robert, ill.  II. Title.
PZ8.3.C99Tic   2012
[E]—dc22

2008051780
CIP
AC

12   13   14   15   LP/WOR     10  9  8  7  6  5  4  3    ❖   First Edition

I Can Read!™

SHARED
**My
First**
READING

# TICK
# TOCK
# CLOCK

A PHONICS
READER

BY
MARGERY CUYLER

PICTURES BY
ROBERT NEUBECKER

**HARPER**

*An Imprint of HarperCollinsPublishers*

Tick tock.

Nine o'clock.

Tick tock.

Knock, knock.

Tick tock.

Ten o'clock.

Tick tock.

Messy smocks.

Tick tock.

Eleven o'clock.

Tick tock.

Falling blocks.

Tick tock.

Twelve o'clock.

Tick tock.

On the dock.

Tick tock.

One o'clock.

Tick tock.

Soaking socks.

Tick tock.

Two o'clock.

16

Tick tock.

Chase a flock.

Tick tock.

Three o'clock.

Tick tock.

Walk a block.

Tick tock.

Four o'clock.

Tick tock.

Undo the lock.

Tick tock.

Five o'clock.

Tick tock.

Cook in the wok.

Tick tock.

Six o'clock.

Tick tock.

Knock, knock.

Tick tock.

Seven o'clock.

Tick tock.

Asleep like a rock!